DATE DUE			
JUL 12, 94			

j398.2   DEUTSCH, Babette, 1895–
           Tales of faraway folk, chosen and re-
           told by Babette Deutsch and Avrahm
           Yarmolinsky. Pictures by Irena Lorento-
           wicz. New York, Harper [1952] 68p.
Related   illus. 2.75
Books in   *1. Fairy tales*
Catalog
Under

           * Collection of ten tales from Central
             Asia and the Caucasus. Ages 8-10.

                                   Title.   D 64

4

TALES OF FARAWAY FOLK

Tales of
FARAWAY FOLK

Chosen and retold by

BABETTE DEUTSCH
and AVRAHM YARMOLINSKY

Pictures by IRENA LORENTOWICZ

HARPER & ROW, PUBLISHERS, NEW YORK AND EVANSTON

For

SALLY AND TOBY

CONTENTS

FOREWORD

On the shores of icy seas, at the edge of forests where wild creatures lurk, in the shadow of savage crags, and on broad plains where as far as the eye can see the only billows are those of the wheat in the wind, live people with few books or none. They work hard, hunting, trapping, and fishing, or caring for the crops, or minding their herds on the hills. But when night comes, they gather round the fire, in their huts or tents, or perhaps out under the stars, and tell stories. One northern tribe has a saying that in ancient times, to keep men from being weary-hearted, a kind god created the storyteller. He is an important figure, but most of the older people can relate the tales, and the younger ones soon learn them. In these pages you will find set down a few that they especially like to tell and to hear.

TALES OF FARAWAY FOLK

THE HAWK AND THE HEN

The peasant's children have finished their chores by gathering the eggs. Now they want grandmother to tell them a story. Here is one that she heard from her grandmother, who heard it from her grandmother, perhaps sitting on the same earthen seat in front of the same whitewashed, thatch-roofed cottage. It is part of a village lying in the midst of the wide wheatfields of the old Ukraine. If the story has been told for so many years by so many knowing old souls, it must be true.

There was a time when the hawk and the hen were friends. And the hawk and the cock were friends, too.

I

Whenever the hawk came to see them and they asked him what he had been doing, he would say:

"Oh, I have been flying up in the sky. You should try it some day. It's great fun!"

The cock wasn't interested.

"I can have plenty of fun down here in the barnyard," he said.

But the hen thought it must be delightful to fly up in the sky, and she begged the hawk to teach her how to do it. So he started giving her lessons. But the hen was slow in learning, and after several lessons she could not even fly to the top of the hedge.

Now the hawk was a prince among birds. And he had everything that a prince should have. Among his treasures were two things of special note. One was a royal red comb such as princes wore in those faraway times. The hawk was not very fond of the royal red comb because he did not think it was truly becoming. The other princely treasure was a necklace of precious pearls. This the hawk valued above everything.

Whenever the hawk came to give the hen a lesson, she would say to herself: "Flying is all very well. But more than anything I should like to own that necklace of precious pearls." After a while she said as much to the cock.

2

"Do you really want that necklace?" he asked.

"Oh, I would do anything to own it," said the hen.

"Very well," said the cock. "The next time the hawk comes to give you a lesson in flying, we'll invite him to stay to dinner. We'll put a bit of henbane into the dessert, just enough to put him to sleep. And when he's asleep, we'll take the necklace away from him. While we're about it, I'll take the royal red comb for myself."

The idea of stealing made the hen a little nervous. She is nervous to this day. But she wanted the necklace so much that she was willing to do anything to get it. So she agreed.

The next time the hawk came, they begged him to stay to dinner. So he did. He ate everything they gave him, and he ate a big helping of dessert, with the henbane in it. He soon dozed off, and when he was fast asleep, the cock stole the necklace of precious pearls and gave it to the hen. While he was about it, he stole the royal red comb, too, and put it on top of his own head. There you can see it to this day. The hen put round her plump neck the necklace of precious pearls.

When the hawk woke up, he discovered his loss. He did not mind losing the royal red comb, because he had never thought it truly becoming. But he valued the princely necklace of precious pearls above everything.

3

When he saw it round the plump neck of the hen, he was furiously angry. He was so angry that he flew at her and snatched the necklace. As he did so, the string broke, and all the precious pearls scattered among the kernels of corn and the gravel in the barnyard.

"Our friendship is over!" screamed the hawk. "I will never give you another lesson. I'm going away. But I'll be back!"

The cock tossed his head, with the royal red comb on it. But the hen was very nervous. She is nervous to this day.

Time passed, and there was no sign of the hawk. After a while the hen began to think that perhaps he had forgiven her.

Meanwhile she had laid a dozen eggs. And in good time she hatched out a dozen chicks. She was so proud and happy that she quite forgot everything else.

One fine summer day she took the chicks for a walk round the barnyard. Whom should she spy but the hawk, flying up in the sky! "I never learned to fly," the hen thought to herself, "and I suppose my chicks won't learn, either. But that doesn't matter. The hawk must have forgiven me, and now he is coming down to admire my chicks."

The hawk did admire the chicks. But he had not for-

given the hen. He swooped down, seized one of the chicks, and flew off with it.

"Chk, chk!" cried the hen, but it did no good. The next day the hawk swooped down again, seized another chick, and flew off with it. On the third day the hawk swooped down, seized a third chick, and flew off with it.

"Chk, chk!" cried the hen. "This will never do! The hawk hasn't forgiven me. And he is revenging himself for the loss of the necklace by stealing my chicks. I must find the pearls that were scattered when the string of the necklace broke. If I gather them all, perhaps then the hawk will forgive me. We shall be friends again, and my chicks will be safe."

So the hen went to work, looking about among the kernels of corn and the gravel in the barnyard, trying to recover the precious pearls. But not one did she find. She goes on picking about among the kernels and the gravel in the barnyard looking for the pearls to this day.

THE ONE WHO WASN'T AFRAID

In the far north lives a hardy tribe of hunters who wander over a vast region extending from the eastern shores of the White Sea to the lower reaches of the Yenisei River in Siberia. They call themselves "Nenetz nenei" which means "real man." Raw meat and fish is their food and they drink the warm blood of the animals they kill. They herd reindeer with the help of dogs, a type of white spitz. When they are not on the move, they set up cone-shaped tents like Indian tepees called "chooms." Here, on bitter Arctic nights, they crouch about the fire and shorten the hours with tales like this.

Once upon a time the dog lived all alone in the forest. But he grew tired of his lonely way of living and went to look for a companion.

He traveled for a long time without meeting anyone. At last he fell in with a hare.

"Good day to you," said the dog.

"Good day," answered the hare.

"Tell me," said the dog, "how would you like to come along with me? We might live very comfortably together. As it is, I am all alone and I lead a dog's life. What do you say?"

"Thank you," replied the hare politely. "I should very much like to stay with you."

So the hare went along with the dog.

They spent a pleasant day together, and when night came they lay down to sleep side by side.

The hare was tired out with leaping about and soon fell asleep, but the dog was not very drowsy. He lay awake thinking how lucky he was to have found someone to share life with him. At last he too fell asleep.

But he had not slept long when he began to dream. He dreamed that he had lost the hare and he began barking in his sleep. The barking woke the hare, and he cried out, "Hush, hush! You will rouse the wolf, and he will come running to eat us up!"

The dog stopped barking, but he was annoyed.

8

"What a timid fellow the hare is!" he thought to himself. "I can't put up with him. I must look for another companion."

When morning came he said to the hare, "Our ways seem to be different. We do not suit one another."

So the two parted company, and the dog went off to look for another friend.

He went a long way without meeting anyone, but at last he fell in with the wolf. The wolf showed no signs of wanting to eat him. On the contrary, he looked like a cousin of the dog's, though of a rather rough sort.

"Good day to you," said the dog.

"Good day," answered the wolf.

"Master Wolf," said the dog, "what do you say to coming to live with me? As it is, I am all alone and I lead a dog's life."

"Very well," said the wolf.

So the wolf went along with the dog.

Night came, and the pair settled down to sleep side by side. The wolf found his new resting-place uncommonly comfortable and soon fell asleep. But the dog was busy with his own thoughts.

"What a fool the hare was!" he said to himself. "The wolf is a fine fellow. He will do me no harm. On the contrary, he is almost one of the family, so to speak. And he is strong. Nothing could scare him!" The mere idea amused the dog, and since he had not learned how to laugh, he began to bark.

The barking woke up the wolf, and he leaped to his feet.

"Be quiet!" he said. "You will rouse the bear, and he will come lumbering through the forest and maul us to death."

The dog said nothing, but he thought to himself, "So the wolf too is a coward! I must get another companion."

When morning came the dog said to the wolf, "If my barking disturbs you, I don't think we'll hit it off together. We had best each go our own ways."

So the two parted company, and the dog went to look for another companion.

He traveled quite a distance and at last whom should he meet but the bear. The bear was a huge roly-poly, and he looked thoroughly good-natured.

"Good day to you," said the dog.

"A very good day," said the bear.

"Friend Bear," said the dog, "how would you like to come and live with me? As it is, I am all alone, and I lead a dog's life. What do you say?"

"That sounds very fine," said the bear. "But tell me, are there any wild bees in your neighborhood?"

"That there are," said the dog. "Swarms of them. You wouldn't mind that, I hope?"

"Not at all," said the bear. "They will make it all the pleasanter for me. Let's go."

So the bear went along with the dog.

Very soon the dog discovered why the bear had asked about the wild bees. He made a good meal of wild honeycomb. As for the dog, he took a light supper of the remains of some bones.

After their meal the two of them went to sleep. The bear was soon snoring, but the dog had not eaten much, and he began to think about what he would like for breakfast.

"A juicy chop would be delicious," he thought to himself. "But that is hard to come by. Perhaps I can bring down a bird. That would make a tasty breakfast." And he began to bark with pleasure.

The noise woke the bear, and he started up, growling.

"Be quiet!" he grumbled. "What do you want to make a racket like that for? You will get the man on our trail, and when he finds us he will shoot us."

The dog said nothing. But he thought to himself, "It seems the bear is afraid, too. I cannot have a coward for a companion. In the morning I must look for someone else."

When morning came, the dog bade the bear farewell, and went off to look for another companion.

He traveled a long while, but nor hide nor hair of another creature did he see. At last he came to the edge of the forest. By this time the dog was very tired and he sat down to rest. As he sat there, he heard a noise nearby. It was not very loud, but it was very steady: hack, hack, hack . . . He pricked up his ears and listened, wondering what it could be. Then he got up to find out.

At the side of a small clearing he saw the man chopping down a tree. The noise he had heard was the sound of the woodcutter's ax.

"Come," said the dog to himself. "Let me have a chat with the man." And he went up to him, wagging his tail.

"Hey, there, pooch!" said the man, before the dog could speak. "What are you doing in this part of the world?"

"I am looking for a companion," said the dog. "As it is, I live all alone and I lead a dog's life."

"That won't do at all," said the man. "Come home with me, and we'll live together. My *choom* is not far off."

13

The dog did not know what the man meant by his *choom*, but he was willing to find out. So he said,

"Thank you. I think I should like that."

It was getting to be dusk. The woodcutter slung his ax over his shoulder, and leaving tomorrow's task for tomorrow, he turned homeward to his *choom*.

When they got there, the dog discovered that this was a large tent with a smoke hole at the top. It was much cozier than any den he had ever seen.

The man promptly set about preparing a meal and set out some food for the dog.

"This is splendid!" thought the dog.

He was very hungry and he ate it all up in a hurry.

The woodcutter was tired after his day's work and he soon lay down asleep. As for the dog, he settled down beside the warm ashes, and fell asleep too.

But he had eaten so much and so fast that he had strange dreams. He dreamed that he was out walking and he met the hare, but the hare heard the wolf rustling among the trees and ran away. Then the dog met the wolf, but the wolf lifted up his head and listened, and suddenly cried out, "The bear is coming!" and ran away. Then the dog went on in his dream and met the bear. But the bear soon said, "We are coming to the clearing and we shall meet the woodcutter. He is a man and carries a gun. He is bound to shoot us." And the bear ran away. The dog went on walking in his dream until he met the woodcutter. He had no gun, only an ax, and the dog was so glad to see him that he began jumping about and barking with delight. It was all a dream, except the bark, and that was real. It was so loud that it woke up the man. It even woke up the dog himself.

"There, there, pup!" said the man. "What are you barking about? There is nothing to be afraid of."

"I know it," answered the dog. "I am only barking because I am glad to be here."

"Stay here, then," said the man, "and keep me company. Only try to do your barking in the daytime."

"That I will," said the dog, and went happily back to sleep.

When he woke in the morning and found himself in the woodcutter's *choom*, and smelled the pleasant fragrance of breakfast cooking, he was so delighted that he did enough barking for the rest of the day and the night too.

"I am staying with you, man," he said. "It is a fine thing to have you for a friend. You are the one creature I have found who is not afraid."

"What is there to be afraid of?" asked the man with a

15

laugh. "Besides, we are a match for anyone now that we are together."

"True enough," said the dog.

So the dog stayed with the man and the pair became the greatest friends. And so they have remained to this day.

SARTAK-PAI

The region of central Asia known as the Altai is one of tower-ing peaks, deep gorges, and swift rivers. The people who live in this wilderness have made up many stories about it. Under the starry skies of a summer night the hunters sit around the fire, and some old man or a blind girl who is respected as a story-teller will recite the tales in singsong. Often the hero of the story is the giant, Sartak-Pai, of whom you will hear now.

High up in the Altai Mountains at the mouth of the river Ini there lived mighty Sartak-Pai. His black pigtail was so long that it touched the ground. His eye-brows were so bushy that they looked like a thicket of brushwood. He was as strong as he was big, and as skill-ful as he was strong. None was so fine a shot as Sartak-Pai: his saddlebags were never empty, and there was always extra fat game strung to his saddle.

He had one son whose name was Adoochee. Nowhere could you find a young man more respectful to his parents. When Adoochee heard from afar the familiar sound of hooves, he ran out swiftly to meet his father and unsaddle his horse. As for Adoochee's wife, Oimok, she busied herself making the old man comfortable. Delicious were the dishes that she prepared for him: eighteen different ways she had of dressing the game that he brought home. Ten various drinks she made for him out of mare's milk.

But though his son and his daughter-in-law were so dutiful, mighty Sartak-Pai was not happy. Day and night he heard the crying of the rivers that were prisoned in the mountains. Tossing from one rock to another, the rivers were torn to shreds. Squeezed between the cliffs, they broke into thin streams. Cruelly blocked and choked, they groaned and they wept. Mighty Sartak-Pai grew weary of seeing their tears and listening to their cries.

"This will never do," he said to himself. "I must free

these rivers. I must clear a way for them so that they can reach the Arctic Ocean."

Thereupon the old man called his son and said to him, "Child, go you to the south, and I shall go to the east. We must free the rivers, so that they will stop wailing, and we must let them go their way to the Arctic Ocean, as is right and proper."

"Very good, father," answered Adoochee obediently.

So he traveled south to Mount Belooha, where it lifts its head among the eternal snows, and began to look for a road for the river Catoon.

As for Sartak-Pai, he went to the east, to a broad lake. With the forefinger of his right hand he opened a channel on the shore of the lake, and a river flowed forth from that spot. And into this river flowed all the nearby brooks and rills, all the springs and underground streams, wailing no longer, but singing the song of free waters.

Mighty Sartak-Pai rejoiced, but through the cheerful din he heard the crying of another river. He stretched forth his left hand and with the forefinger of that hand he drew a furrow for the unhappy river. And the waters running away from the rocks that had clasped them laughed aloud. And the mighty old man laughed with them.

"Such work should not be done with the left hand," he muttered. "But it is good that I can work with my left hand, too."

Then Sartak-Pai stretched forth his right hand again and made a path for the river that lay bound in the hills beyond, so that it could flow freely down the slopes.

But when this labor was completed, the mighty old man had time to sit down and think.

"Where is my son?" he asked himself. "Why doesn't he meet me?" Then he summoned the bird with spotted wings.

"Fly off, my good bird," he said. "Find Adoochee and see how he is faring."

The bird with spotted wings flew off to the south to Mount Belooha, where he found the river Catoon, and followed its course westward. At last he overtook young Adoochee. He was busy leading the river Catoon farther to the west.

"What in the world are you doing, Adoochee?" asked the bird. "You have lost your bearings! And when will you ever meet your father? He is waiting for you!"

"What a dunderhead I am!" cried Adoochee, hastily turning the course of the river Catoon to the east. "Tell my father I will meet him in three days."

The bird hurried back to the old man.

"Mighty Sartak," he said, "your son will be with you in three days."

At these words Sartak-Pai beamed.

"My good bird," he answered, "you have done my bidding and summoned my son. Now I shall reward you fittingly. I shall teach you how to have food in plenty forever and a day. Do not look for worms in the earth. Do not seek for gnats among the branches. Perch on a tree trunk and hold tight with your claws, knock at the bark with your beak, and shout, 'Kiuk, kiuk! The son of the khan is celebrating his wedding. Put on your robes of yellow silk and your caps of black beaver! Hurry, hurry! The son of the khan invites you to this wedding!' And all the worms and the gnats and the other insects will crawl quickly out from between the wrinkles of the bark into the open. And you shall have your fill of them."

From that day to this the woodpecker gets his food just as old Sartak-Pai taught him.

During the three days that the old man was waiting for his son to arrive, he pressed his forefinger upon the nearest valley. And in the hollow made by his finger a lake collected.

At last the three days were up and Adoochee appeared, leading the river Catoon.

"It is good that you are here at last, my son," said Sartak-Pai. "Now come with me."

Then out of the lake that he had just made he drew the river Bee. And as Sartak-Pai walked along, drawing the river Bee after him, his son moved swiftly, leading the river Catoon. Not one step did he lag behind his mighty father. So the two moved on toward the great river Ob. At one and the same time father and son led their twin rivers into the wide Ob. And the river Ob carried the waters of the Altai mountains into the Arctic Ocean.

Adoochee stood there proud and happy to think that he had helped his father in the great task of freeing the rivers so that they might flow merrily into the sea.

But Sartak-Pai did not appear quite content.

"Son," he said to the young man, "you have done well in bringing the river Catoon here so quickly. But I must take a look and see if you have traced its course properly, so that people can make good use of it."

So Sartak-Pai walked from the river Ob back along the banks of the river Catoon. Adoochee walked behind him, his knees shaking with fear. Suppose his father were not satisfied! Swiftly Sartak-Pai moved across the land until he came to a steep mountain, one peak in a high range. Then indeed his face grew dark. He frowned so that his eyebrows, fierce as thickets of brushwood, hid

22

his eyes. That was lucky, or his angry glance might have pierced poor Adoochee where he stood quaking.

"Oh, shame and disgrace, Adoochee, my son!" cried Sartak-Pai. "Why have you given the river Catoon a twist here? Men will not thank you for it when they want to use this river. You have done ill, my son."

"Father," pleaded Adoochee, "you must not blame me. I could not split this steep mountain. Even to draw a furrow along the range was too much for me."

At that the old man took the iron bow that was slung across his shoulder and fitted it with a three-sided arrow of flashing brass. He pulled the string and the arrow sped from the bow.

The steep mountain split in two. Half of it dropped into a valley and was at once covered with a cloak of tall pine trees. The other half is still towering above the river Catoon. And even now men praise mighty Sartak for having mended Catoon's course so that it is straight as the path of an arrow.

Then father and son traveled farther along the course of the Catoon. Suddenly Sartak-Pai halted. They had come to a spot where the river was tearing and clawing at its banks like a wild animal. The waters rushed by in a fierce torrent.

"This is not right," said Sartak. "How will men cross such a torrent, my son?" he asked.

He sat down on a rock beside the wild waters and thought and thought. At last he spoke.

"Son," he said, "we must have a bridge here. There's no other way out."

Young Adoochee made no answer. He was so tired that he stood before his father swaying on his feet like tall grass waving in the wind.

"Go off and rest for a spell," said Sartak, kindly. "But see that you do not fall asleep. And do not let your wife close her eyes, either, out of respect for my labors."

"Will you be working all night, Father?" asked Adoochee, in wonder.

"When there are great labors to be performed," answered Sartak sternly, "sleep does not dare come near."

So Adoochee went off. And Sartak-Pai began to collect heaps of rock in the skirt of his greatcoat. He worked all day long without pause, and when night came he went on working.

The river Catoon rushed by like a madman. The wind shrieked. The trees groaned. Black clouds were crowding aloft. A small cloud bumped into a large cloud and as they struck, lightning flashed forth. Sartak stretched out his arm and caught the lightning and set it in the split stem of a fir tree. By the glare of the lightning he began to build the bridge.

He took one stone after another from the skirt of his greatcoat and set it firmly on its fellow. Stone after stone he put in its place, until only a few yards of the river were still to be bridged.

And then suddenly the bridge collapsed!

Sartak-Pai roared like an angry bear. He dropped the skirt of his greatcoat and the rest of the rocks tumbled into the water. They fell with a terrific rumble and strewed the bed of the river so thickly that the water hurls itself over them with hissing clamor and boiling foam to this day.

Meanwhile, young Adoochee, resting while his father worked, had fallen asleep, and his wife as well. The thunder of the falling rocks woke them both up. They were so fearful of the wrath of Sartak-Pai that they turned into gray geese and flew away.

Sartak-Pai saw them flying and in his rage he picked up a boulder and hurled it at them. The boulder fell upon the steppe and there it can be seen even to this day. As for Adoochee and his wife, they were so scared that they remained geese ever after.

Sad and lonely, old Sartak-Pai mounted his horse and returned to his home at the mouth of the river Ini. There

was no one there to welcome him, no one busy preparing food and drink for him. There was no one to unsaddle his horse for him. Sartak had to do the work himself.

He took off the saddle and then he removed the felt that kept it from chafing the horse's back. The felt was damp with sweat, for it was no easy thing to carry the mighty Sartak-Pai. The old man threw the piece of felt on a cliff to dry. But then he bethought him that the cliff was in the shadow and the felt would not dry quickly enough. So he took up the cliff and moved it into the sunshine. Then he sat down beside it and took his long-earned rest.

A CLEVER JUDGE

The people who tell this tale live on the vast steppes or prairies of southwestern Asia. They are herders of cattle, sheep, and goats. And they are clever fellows, too, as you shall see.

There lived a man in the steppes who was famous for his justice and wisdom. At that time if a man was known for his fairness, people came to him from far and wide to ask him to settle their disputes. And so it

28

was that one day two villagers appeared before this wise man and asked him to settle their quarrel.

"Tell me your story," the judge said to the plaintiff.

"I had to leave my village," said the plaintiff, "for I had business elsewhere. And all my wealth was a hundred gold coins. I did not come by them easily. I had to work hard for them, and I did not want them to be stolen while I was away. Nor did I care to carry so much money with me on my journey. So I entrusted these gold coins for safekeeping to this man here. When I got back from my journey, he denied that he had ever received the money from me."

"And who saw you give him these hundred gold coins?" asked the judge.

"No one saw it. We went together to the heart of the forest and there I handed him the coins."

"What have you to say to this?" the judge asked, turning to the defendant.

The defendant shrugged his shoulders.

"I don't know what he is talking about," said the man. "I never went to the forest with him. I never saw his gold coins."

"Do you remember the place where you handed over the money?" the judge asked the plaintiff.

29

"Of course I do. It was under a tall oak. I remember it very well. I can point it out with no trouble at all."

"So you do have a witness, after all," said the judge. "Here, take my signet ring, go to the tall tree under which you stood when you handed over the money, set the seal of my signet ring against the trunk, and bid the tree appear before me to bear out the truth of your story."

The plaintiff took the signet ring and went off to carry out the demand of the judge. The defendant remained behind and waited for his return.

After some time had passed, the judge turned to the defendant and asked, "Do you think he has reached the oak by this time?"

"No, not yet," was the answer.

After further time had passed, the judge again turned to the defendant and asked, "Do you think he has reached the tree by this time?"

"Yes," was the answer, "by now he must have reached it."

Not long after that the plaintiff returned.

"Well?" asked the judge.

"I did just as you said," replied the plaintiff. "I walked as far as the forest and then I went on until I came to the tall oak under which we stood when I handed over my gold coins. I set the seal of your signet ring against the trunk of the tree and I bade it appear before you as a witness. But the tree refused to budge."

"Never mind," said the judge. "The oak has appeared before me and it has borne witness in your favor."

At that the defendant exclaimed, "How can you say such a thing! I have been here all this while and no tree has stalked into the place."

"But," replied the judge, "you said that you had not been in the forest at all. And yet when I asked you whether the plaintiff had reached the oak, first you answered that he could not have reached it, and the second time you said that he must surely have reached it. Therefore, you *were* in the forest and you remembered where the oak was under which you stood when the plaintiff handed his gold coins to you for safekeeping. Now you must not only return him his hundred gold pieces, but you must also pay a fine for having tried to cheat him."

So the tree was a witness without budging, and justice was done.

31

THE MISERLY FROG

The storytellers of the Altai often relate the mighty doings of giants. But they also tell such tales as this.

Once upon a time there was a frog who lived in a round pond. She was well content with the round pond, but one day she thought she would go for a walk. And so, plop-plop, out she hopped, and plop-plop, down the road she went.

After she had gone some distance the frog got tired.

"It is time to go home to my round pond," she said to herself.

So she turned about and, plop-plop, went toward her own house. But she had not gone far when she saw that she had lost her way.

And that was not all. She was on the path to an ant hill. That was a sad thing. Dozens of ants began to run all over her back. Hundreds of ants began to bite her.

"Oh, oh, oh!" cried the frog. "Aren't you ashamed to bite a person who has lost her way? Aren't you ashamed to suck the blood of the hungry?"

The ants were ashamed. They stopped running over her back. They stopped biting her. Instead, they bowed low before her, and said, "Honored frog, be our guest! Come home with us to our ant hill. Eat our food, drink our mead."

"Thank you," said the frog. "I shall be glad to come."

So she went to the ants' house. They gave her good things to eat. They gave her mead to drink. She ate and she drank. She drank and she ate. What she ate she did not remember. What she said at table she did not know. What she slept on after the feast she could not guess. So much had she eaten, so much had she drunk!

In the morning the frog woke up, and said to herself, "It is time for me to go home to my round pond."

33

Then she turned to one of the ants and said politely, "Be so good as to climb up that tree. When you get to the top, look here and look there, and see if you can find my home. It is a round pond."

The ant obliged the frog. She climbed up the tree. She looked here. She looked there. Then she climbed down again.

"I can tell you," she said to the frog, "that there is a round pond gleaming in the sun yonder in the west. If you like, I will show you the short cut to it."

"You are very kind," said the frog, joyfully. "Come with me and I will prepare a treat for you. Let's go quickly."

"Not so fast," answered the ant. "I can't be your guest all by myself. Yesterday we all dined you and wined you. It would seem proper that today you should invite all of us. And besides, we don't know how to work alone or how to play alone or how to eat and drink alone. We are that sort, we do everything together."

"Very well," said the frog. And she invited all the ants to go home with her to the round pond. She began traveling along, plop-plop, and the ants followed after her in a mighty stream.

All the ants in the ant hill, and all the ants in a second

ant hill, and all the ants in a thousand ant hills, went along to visit the frog.

At last they came to the round pond.

"You wait here," said the frog to the ants, "and I will go and give orders about the party." And she jumped into the water.

The ants stood on the bank and waited for her to return. A whole day passed by, but the frog did not show herself. Another day passed, and still there was no sign of the frog. The ants waited and waited, and so seven days passed by.

On the seventh day the queen ant got angry.

"Well!" she cried. "While we wait for the frog's party, we shall all die of hunger."

Then she tightened her belt around her empty middle and started for home. All the ants tightened their belts and followed her.

Ever since then the ants go about with their middles tightly belted. They haven't filled out from that day to this.

THE GULL

"The country of the north" that you will hear about in this story is part of Karelia, which borders on Finland and on the White Sea. It is a land of lakes and rivers that freeze over in winter, so that you can travel across the ice on a sleigh. In the warm season the many islands are bright with willow trees and birches. There are forests, too, where bears and wolves abound. The people do not tell their stories: they sing them. And they believe that songs can work magic.

Long, long ago in the country of the north there lived an old witch. Her name was Heesee. She was twisted like a withered old branch and she was very ugly. But old Heesee had an only daughter who was tall and straight and lovely to look at. Her name was Katerina. Many were the young men who wanted to marry Katerina, but ugly old Heesee demanded a better husband for her daughter than any of them.

Now the smith Ilmarinen had heard of the beauty of Katerina. He thought it would be a fine thing to have such a girl for his wife. He was young and strong and handsome and the most famous smith that ever worked at the forge. So he thought he might try his luck.

"Bring me my greatcoat with a thousand buttons," he said to his mother. "I am going to the North Country to woo the beautiful Katerina."

His mother smiled at her son and brought him the greatcoat with the thousand buttons, and each of the thousand buttons shone like new minted silver.

"Set six golden cuckoos with golden voices on the shaft-bow of the sleigh," said Ilmarinen to his mother. "They must sing a golden song so my bride-to-be may hear me coming."

His mother smiled at her son and quickly fetched six golden cuckoos with golden voices and set them on the shaft-bow of his sleigh so that Katerina could hear their song and know that Ilmarinen was coming to woo her even before she saw him.

But Ilmarinen had one serious rival. That was the Sun. In fact, the Sun was so deeply in love with Katerina that he had eyes for no one else. The people of the North Country felt colder than ever when the Sun left them to stare only at Katerina. They complained long and loud. Ilmarinen the smith heard their teeth chattering and heard them groaning as he drove toward old Heesee's house.

"You're behaving very badly," he said to the Sun. "You look only at Katerina. All the rest of the North Country is left in darkness and cold. I'll put an end to this. Shine on all alike! Otherwise I'll go to my smithy and forge another sun, a sun that will give light to everybody. Then what will you do?"

When the Sun heard Ilmarinen the smith talk this way he got scared. He stopped looking only at Katerina. He shone once more for all alike.

As for the old witch Heesee, when she found that Ilmarinen the smith could make the Sun behave, she decided that he was just the husband for her daughter Katerina.

Up he drove in his sleigh, the six golden cuckoos sing-

38

ing with their golden voices, and all the thousand buttons on his greatcoat shining like new minted silver. And the old witch Heesee lost no time in preparing for the wedding.

As soon as the ceremony was over, Ilmarinen tucked his bride into his sleigh, and started on the drive home. It was a good long drive between old Heesee's house and the home of Ilmarinen the smith. The ground was covered with snow, and the sleigh had to travel over frozen lakes and rivers.

Now the beautiful Katerina did not want to be the wife of a smith, even the most famous smith that ever worked at the forge. All day long, she thought, he would be in his smithy, hammering away noisily. A man who can threaten to forge another sun is no ordinary smith, and he would make no ordinary noise. And, of course, he would be black with soot. Ilmarinen was no ordinary smith, and he wouldn't have ordinary soot on his hands and face. The more Katerina thought about it, the less she liked the idea of being his wife.

As they drove on they came upon the tracks of a hare. "I would rather follow the tracks of a hare," Katerina said to herself, "than be the wife of the smith!"

They drove farther, and soon they came upon the

39

tracks of a wolf. "I would rather follow the tracks of a wolf," Katerina said to herself, "than be the wife of the smith!"

They drove farther, and soon they came upon the tracks of a bear. "I would rather follow the tracks of a bear," Katerina said to herself, "than be the wife of the smith!"

But Katerina was not a witch's daughter for nothing.

They had not driven much farther when all of a sudden the shaft-bow broke. All six golden cuckoos flew away. Ilmarinen raised his eyebrows, and Katerina jumped out of the sleigh onto the frozen lake.

"Wait a bit," said Ilmarinen. And swiftly he sang an island onto the lake, and sang a whole grove of willow trees onto the island. Out of the willow wood he made a fine shaft-bow. So Katerina got grumpily into the sleigh again and they drove on.

But they had not driven much farther when all of a sudden the shafts of the sleigh broke. Ilmarinen raised his eyebrows, and Katerina jumped out of the sleigh onto the frozen river.

"Wait a bit," said Ilmarinen. And swiftly he sang another island onto the river, and sang a whole grove of birch trees onto the island. Out of the birches he made

40

two strong shafts. So Katerina got grumpily into the sleigh again and they drove on.

But they had not driven much farther when all of a sudden one of the runners broke. Ilmarinen raised his eyebrows, and Katerina jumped out of the sleigh onto the snow.

"Wait a bit," said Ilmarinen. And swiftly he sang his forge onto the snow. Then he took off his greatcoat with the thousand buttons, so he could set to work and forge a new runner.

But this time Katerina did not wait. While Ilmarinen was bent over the forge she ran away.

When Ilmarinen had forged the new runner, he put on his greatcoat with the thousand buttons, and looked around for Katerina. She was nowhere to be seen.

By that time it was night. "Perhaps," he thought to himself, "she has hidden herself among the stars. There are so many that she thinks I shall never find her."

He counted the stars. They were all there, right enough. But Katerina was not among them.

By the time he had finished counting, it was morning. "Perhaps," he thought to himself, "she has hidden herself among the fish in the sea. They dart about so that she thinks I shall never find her."

He counted the fish in the sea. They were all there, right enough. But Katerina was not among them.

By the time he had finished counting, it was afternoon. "Perhaps," he thought to himself, "she has hidden herself among the beasts of the forest." So he turned his steps in that direction. But he had no luck there either.

"No matter," said Ilmarinen the smith. "I am not going to hunt for Katerina any longer. She is not among the stars, or the fishes, or the beasts of the forest. But I know what I have to do."

So he began to sing. And as he sang Katerina was drawn out of hiding, and forced to come and listen.

Ilmarinen went on singing. As he sang, Katerina felt herself change. She was no longer a beautiful girl. She had wings instead of arms. She had a beak instead of a mouth. And when she wanted to speak, she could only cry hoarsely. Ilmarinen had turned her into a sea gull.

"You did not want to be my companion," said Ilmarinen. "Very well. You shall be a sea gull for always and always. You shall live neither on the earth nor in the sea. You shall be hated by the fishermen because you tear their nets. You shall make your way over the waste waters: there you shall fly and there you shall go crying."

From that day to this the gull flies over the waters.

42

And when a storm rises and the whitecaps tumble roughly you hear the gull crying. But she is not crying about the coming storm. She is mourning her lost happiness.

THE THOROUGHBRED

If you had been born to an Ossete family living on a slope of the Caucasian Range, north or south, your home would have been a flat-roofed cabin, where the fire on which the pot was boiling was always filling the room with smoke. In winter your mountain village would have been snowbound. The long cold evenings would be the time for stories. You would huddle near the fire for warmth, and your mother would have to keep wiping her eyes that were tearing with the smoke. But nothing would matter as long as she went on with the story. The Ossetes, like other natives of the Caucasus, are great horsemen. As often as not her story would be about horses.

There lived a man in a mountain village who had only one son. Now this son, a fine little lad, was kidnapped

44

when he was very young. The boy's father wasted no time lamenting the loss of his son, but rode in search of him. All in vain. The boy had been taken far from his home and sold to the chief of a distant tribe. The chief made a shepherd of him.

One day as the boy was following his herd, he came upon a horse's skull. He examined it carefully and then he wept long and bitterly. A passer-by noticed the shepherd lad crying over the horse's skull.

"Why do you cry, boy?" he asked.

"Ah," said the boy, "I cry because this is not the skull of a common horse, but of a thoroughbred, one of those beauties who race with the wind." But he did not tell the stranger that he wept because he was reminded of home, and of his father, who had taught him the family secret: how to recognize these rare creatures.

The stranger told the chief that he had found his shepherd crying over a horse's skull as over the body of his own brother.

"If you can recognize a thoroughbred by his skull, you must also be able to tell a living one," the chief said to the boy.

"Yes, indeed," he answered.

"That is a great gift," the chief thought to himself.

And he took the shepherd boy into his own house, and brought him up with his own children.

45

"The day will come," the chief told him, "when you will find a thoroughbred for me."

But as often as he repeated this, the boy replied that such wonderful horses were as rare as summer snow. You must travel the world over to find them, and examine drove after drove, and still your search might be in vain.

Nevertheless, the chief was determined to possess such a remarkable animal. So one fine day he took the boy, and the pair of them set out to find a thoroughbred.

They traveled far and met with many a splendid drove of horses, but not one animal that had all the fine points of a perfect thoroughbred. Finally they came upon a drove in which there was a raven-black horse without a single light hair in his coat. He was a beauty.

"Purchase this stallion, master, at any price," the boy advised.

"Is this a thoroughbred?" asked the chief.

"It is a fine horse," was all that the boy would answer.

So the chief bought the raven-black stallion. They went farther, and came upon a beautiful mare. Her coat was raven-black except for a small white star on her forehead and another on one of her hind legs.

"Purchase this mare, master, at any price," the boy advised.

47

"Is she a thoroughbred?" asked the chief.

"She is a fine horse," was all that the boy would answer.

So the chief bought the mare, and with these two horses they returned home.

But the chief was troubled.

"I have two magnificent horses," he said to himself. "But this boy can ride like no other. Perhaps he will take one of them and ride away and then I shall not see him or the horse again."

Unable to bear his suspicion, he made the boy take an oath that he would not run away.

"I swear," vowed the boy, "that I will not leave you until you yourself bid me do so. When you say to me, 'Be off with you!' then I will depart, and not until then."

The chief was satisfied. Soon after that they started to break in the horses.

One day after the horses had been broken in, the chief told the boy to saddle them, for they were to go riding.

"The mare is the more beautiful animal," said the boy, "with that white star on her forehead and on her hind leg."

"I will ride the mare," said the chief. "You mount the black stallion."

48

So they set out together. They had not gone far when the boy began to do stunt riding. He galloped too close to his master. He trotted directly in front of him. He annoyed him in a dozen ways. The chief bore with him for a time, but at last he lost patience and shouted, "Be off with you!"

At that the boy spurred the black stallion and dashed away. Too late the chief realized the mistake he had made. He gave chase promptly, but the mare did not gain an inch on the black stallion. They rode on and on, but the two horses kept an even distance.

Finally the boy turned into a dry river bed full of stones. The chief followed. But this test was too severe for the mare. The leg with the white star proved weak. She began to fall back. The stallion galloped on over the stones. The mare could not keep up. At last, seeing that it was useless to follow, the chief turned the mare about and went sadly home.

But the boy rode on and on, far into the hills, until he came to a mountain village. It was high time to rest. He leaped from his black stallion, and tethered him to a post in front of a small house. Glad to be freed of his burden, the black stallion neighed loudly.

A sturdy old man came out of the house.

"That is the neighing of a thoroughbred!" he exclaimed.

He was about to stroke the nose of the black stallion when he saw the boy who had ridden him.

"My son! My son!" cried the old man, and took the boy in his arms.

"How did you know me, Father, after all these years?" asked the boy, when the first rejoicings were over.

"Who but a son of mine would find a thoroughbred?" replied his father. "You learned the secret that I taught you. And even as you knew the best horse in the world, so did I know at a glance the best of sons!"

THE OWL'S PUNISHMENT

This is one of the stories told by the Yakuts, who are mostly hunters and trappers, and who live in eastern Siberia. Its vast reaches hold some of the coldest places on earth.

When winter approached the shores of the Arctic Ocean, the birds who had lived there comfortably during the summer began to shiver and shake.

"When it gets really cold we shall all die," they cried to one another.

Finally they decided to choose a master, some strong and clever bird who would know where to take them when winter came.

"Let the crane be our master," said some.

But the duck objected, "If we fly wherever he bids us, we shall be lost."

The widgeon got up and protested. "Surely the crane should be our master! Look at his dignified head, his piercing eyes, his powerful body, his long, strong legs!"

"No," said the duck, "he is a fine fellow. But he is not wise enough to lead us."

Then the swan spoke up. "Let the eagle be our master. Where will you find another bird as fierce and lordly as the eagle? He has eyes that can stare into the sun itself. And he is so strong! The eagle should rule over us."

The duck agreed to this, and the others also. So they made the eagle king over all the birds, and he is so still.

Annoyed at the widgeon because he had not at once recognized his lordliness, the eagle punished him by making him carry the duck on his back. Then he said,

"I must have food for the journey. Some of you must be sacrificed so that I can have strength to lead you to a safe place."

It was decided that the bulfinch should be sacrificed. When he objected, the eagle said firmly, "There are

53

those who eat and those who are eaten. You should be glad to serve your king in this fashion." So that was settled.

Then the eagle commanded the teal to go forth to look for a land of warmth and plenty. The teal wandered far and wide, but no green thing was to be seen. He returned without a word of comfort.

Thereupon the eagle bade the owl seek a warm refuge for the birds. So the owl flew off. After some time he too returned and reported to the eagle that he had had no luck.

"And what a tiresome trip I had!" murmured the owl. "I really need rest." And he settled down cosily beside his wife.

But the teal had noticed a queer glint in the owl's eye. And he hid near the owl's home and listened carefully to hear what he could hear. In a little while he heard the owl talking quietly to his wife.

"My dear," said the owl, "this is a secret between you and me. I do not want everybody to know. But I did find a green place, a warm place, a fine place, beside a sea that never freezes. Oh, what a beautiful country! The air is as soft as your throat feathers. There is no winter there from year's end to year's end."

"Really!" exclaimed his wife. "But why didn't you tell the eagle?"

"Oh, if I had told him about it," replied the owl, "then he would have had all the birds of the Arctic fly there, and the place would get so crowded that there would be no bearing it. When nobody is looking, you and I will fly there quite by ourselves."

When the teal heard this, he cried out. Then he flew to the eagle to tell him the news.

At once the eagle summoned the owl and forced him to tell the truth about the warm country he had found and how it was to be reached. All the birds were delighted, and with joyful cries they set off. All but the owl and his wife.

The owl said to his wife, "Old woman, take good care of the down on your shinbones! You will have need of it. For you and I are not allowed to go to the green land that I found. We shall have to winter here in this cold land."

The owl's wife sighed and smoothed the down on her shinbones. And the owl and his wife winter in the Arctic to this day.

THE WOLF

Little Red Riding Hood would not have had much to fear from the wolf in this story. It is one of the tales current among the Lithuanians, who live in the thickly forested and marshy lands east of the Baltic Sea.

Having worked all morning long, a field hand got tired and sat down to have his noonday meal. While he was sitting there, munching, a wolf came out of the forest, and trotting up to the field hand, he asked, "What are you eating, man?"

56

"Rye bread," answered the field hand.

"Let me taste it," begged the wolf.

The field hand broke off a piece of bread and gave it to the wolf.

"That tastes good!" said the wolf, licking his chops. "I'd like to have some of that whenever I get hungry. But I don't know how to get it. Tell me what to do."

So the man began to teach the wolf how to get bread.

"First you must plow the land," he said.

"Then I'll have bread?" asked the wolf.

"No, wait," said the man. "Then you must harrow the land . . ."

"And then I can eat the bread?" asked the wolf.

"Oh, no, wait. After you've worked the land, you must sow the grain . . ."

"And then I'll have bread?" asked the wolf eagerly.

"Not so fast," said the man. "You must let the grain winter in the ground. In the spring there will be green sprouts. And by the middle of summer the rye will be tall . . ."

"Oh, then I'll have rye bread!" exclaimed the wolf.

"No, indeed, my friend," said the man. "First you must reap the rye and tie it up into sheaves and gather the sheaves into ricks. Then you let the wind blow through

57

them and air them, and the sun shine on them and dry them, and then you take them to the threshing floor."

"Good," said the wolf. "Then I'll eat my fill of bread!"

"Not so," said the man. "The sheaves have to be threshed, the grain gathered and taken to the mill, and there it is ground and made into flour."

"At last I shall eat the bread!" cried the wolf.

"Wait a bit," said the man. "The flour must be made into dough, and then you must give the dough time to rise, and then you must bake it . . ."

"And then it will be bread?" asked the wolf, doubtfully.

"Yes," said the man. "Then it will be good rye bread. And you can eat till you are full."

The wolf grew thoughtful. At last he shook his head and said slowly, "That is hard work and it takes a long time. No, I must do without bread. Tell me a quick and easy way to get food."

"If you don't want to wait for bread," said the man, "just go to the pasture. There you will see a mare with a young colt. The colt has tender flesh. Eat the colt."

"Good," answered the wolf. And he went loping off to the pasture, where the mare was browsing and her colt stood beside her.

But when the colt saw the wolf it got frightened and

hid under its mother's belly. Nevertheless, the wolf made a leap for the colt. But at once the mare threw out her hooves and gave the wolf such a wallop that he was knocked down. Up he got, and tried to attack the colt again, but this time the mare kicked the wolf in the teeth.

Sadly the wolf slunk off and went back to the field hand.

"What shall I do?" he asked. "That mare is much too much for me. I can't get the better of her. I shall never be able to feast on the colt."

"Oh, well," said the man, "if you can't get the colt, go to the meadow. There you will find some sheep grazing. Choose a ram, a fat juicy one, and eat him."

"Good," said the wolf, and went loping off to the meadow.

When he got there he saw a large fat ram. He did not attack the ram, but went quietly up to him and said, "The man has given me permission to eat you up."

The ram made no objections.

"If that's how it is," said the ram, "that's how it must be. If the man has given you permission to eat me, what can I do? But I have one favor to ask."

"I shall grant it gladly if I can," said the wolf.

"Don't rip up my hide and eat me piecemeal. Swallow

me whole. That will be more comfortable for me, and you will be fed just the same."

"Very well," said the wolf agreeably. "How shall we proceed?"

"Nothing easier," said the ram. "You stand over there by the fence with your feet firmly planted, and open your mouth as wide as you can. I'll come running toward you and jump down your throat."

"You won't run in the other direction?" asked the wolf suspiciously.

"No, indeed!" the ram assured him.

"Word of honor?" insisted the wolf.

"Word of honor!" said the ram.

So the wolf went over to the fence, planted his paws firmly on the ground, and opened his mouth as wide as ever he could. Then suddenly the ram came running at him with all his might. He ran so fast and so hard that he gave the wolf a stunning blow on the nose. The wolf fell down in a heap. As for the ram, he went quietly off and hid.

When the wolf finally came to his senses, it was nearly nightfall. He moved his head stiffly from side to side. Then he got up and shook himself all over.

He looked around. Nor hide, nor hair of a living creature was to be seen.

"I certainly saw him running toward me!" muttered the wolf. "And he looked like such a big fat juicy ram. Appearances are deceitful. Perhaps I should have chewed him up piecemeal, instead of swallowing him whole. As it is, I don't feel as though I'd had a morsel to eat."

GRANDFATHER'S ADVICE

This story has long been a favorite with fathers, and even more with grandfathers. It is one of the folktales of the Lettish peasants who since time out of mind have been farming the land south of the Gulf of Riga.

When the world was young and new, people thought everything should be young and new. And so when a man got old, and could not do his share of work any longer, they had no use for him.

63

It was the custom to get rid of those old fellows who were only a burden.

Now there was a man who had an old father and a little son. The grandfather was very feeble. Indeed he scarcely moved from his place near the stove.

"The old man is useless," the man said to himself. "And he seems to have no idea of dying. I shall have to get rid of him."

So he took his little son's sled and piled the old grandfather onto it.

"What are you doing with Grandfather?" asked the little boy.

"I am putting him on your sled. Have you no eyes?" said the man grumpily.

"But where are you taking him?" asked the little boy.

"To the forest," said the man.

"Whatever for?" asked the little boy.

"Never mind," said the man. Although it was such a sensible thing to do, he did not quite like the idea of getting rid of the old grandfather.

"Let me come along!" begged the little boy.

"Be off with you!" said the man. "And stop bothering me with your foolish questions."

"Please let me come along," begged the little boy.

"Please! I won't ask another question. But please let me come!"

"Imp that you are, come if you must," said the man angrily.

So the little boy hopped along after the sled, taking many short steps to the man's big ones, and careful not to ask another question.

Finally they came to the forest. The man dropped the rope with which he had been pulling the sled, shrugged his shoulders, shook his head, and turned around to go home. It seemed a hard thing to leave the old grandfather there in the forest to die, but that was the custom. And who is brave enough to go against custom?

But his little son tugged at his coat.

"You mustn't leave Grandfather here in the forest," he said in a small voice. "He will surely die."

"He is too old to work," said the man. "It is the only sensible thing to do." And he began marching homeward. The little boy ran after him, and pulled at his coat.

"What's the matter now?" the man asked grumpily.

"Daddy," said the little boy. "You mustn't leave my sled there!"

"And why not?" asked the man.

"Because when you are old and worn out, I'll need the sled to carry you to the forest!"

65

"Perhaps," the man said to himself, "I haven't done such a sensible thing after all. When I get old, my son will do with me as I have done with his grandfather."

This displeased him quite as much as the idea of leaving the old grandfather in the forest. So he turned to his son and said, "You are right. And I was wrong. We'll go and fetch Grandfather home again."

So he went back to fetch the sled and the grandfather. But he did not let the neighbors know that he had brought the old man home again. After all, he was going against custom, and that is a risky thing to do. So he hid the old grandfather away in the cellar, and took him food and drink in secret.

Now it happened that not long afterward there was a famine in the land. There were seven years of bad harvest. Certainly nobody was going to be bothered feeding the old codgers. Nobody but this one man. He kept on taking food to the old grandfather in his hiding place. But he took smaller and smaller portions. The old grandfather noticed this, but he said nothing.

The famine was a terrible one. People ate up every crumb of food they could get. They ate their wheat down to the very last grain and they ate their rye down to the very last grain, and when it was time for sowing, there was not even seed grain left in the bins. Nobody knew what to do next. If they had not got rid of the old men, they might have asked advice from them. But the wisdom of the old had died with them.

One day the man who had kept his old father hidden took him his dinner with a sorry face. The dinner was nothing but a piece of bread. And it was a very small piece. It was not fine wheaten bread. It was not even tasty rye bread. It was coarse bread made of barley flour.

"Ah," sighed the old grandfather. "I am very hungry. But I don't know that I can eat this barley bread. I have the stomach for it right enough. But I haven't the teeth for it. I don't ask for fine wheaten bread. But a piece of rye bread now, that would be tasty! Even a very little piece."

"There is famine," said the man. "There is no rye flour to make bread with. There is not even a grain of rye left for sowing."

"Well," said the old grandfather. "That's bad, but it could be worse. You still have a roof of thatch on your threshing barn I suppose. Take the old straw off half the roof and thresh it well. You'll find quite a little grain has been left in the thatch."

The man did as the old grandfather advised, took half the thatch off the roof, threshed the straw, and got a whole jugful of grain. Then he went to tell the old grandfather about it.

"That's good, but it could be better," said the old grandfather. "Put back the threshed thatch, take the other half off the roof, thresh that, and you will get another jugful of grain."

The man did as the old grandfather advised, and it happened just as he had said it would. Then he went to the old grandfather and told him about it.

"Good," said the grandfather. "Plant your grain. Perhaps you will get a crop."

And so the man did, and in good time he got a fine crop of rye.

When the neighbors discovered his good fortune, they came crowding around to ask him how he had come by his seed grain.

"I got good advice from my old father," said the man.

"How could that be?" they asked. "You have no father!"

"Oh, but I have!" he answered. And he brought the old man out of hiding.

"That's my grandfather!" said the boy proudly.

After that nobody thought of getting rid of the old men. They were respected for their wisdom, which the old keep just as the thatch keeps the seeds.